Discarded

Socks for Mr Wolf

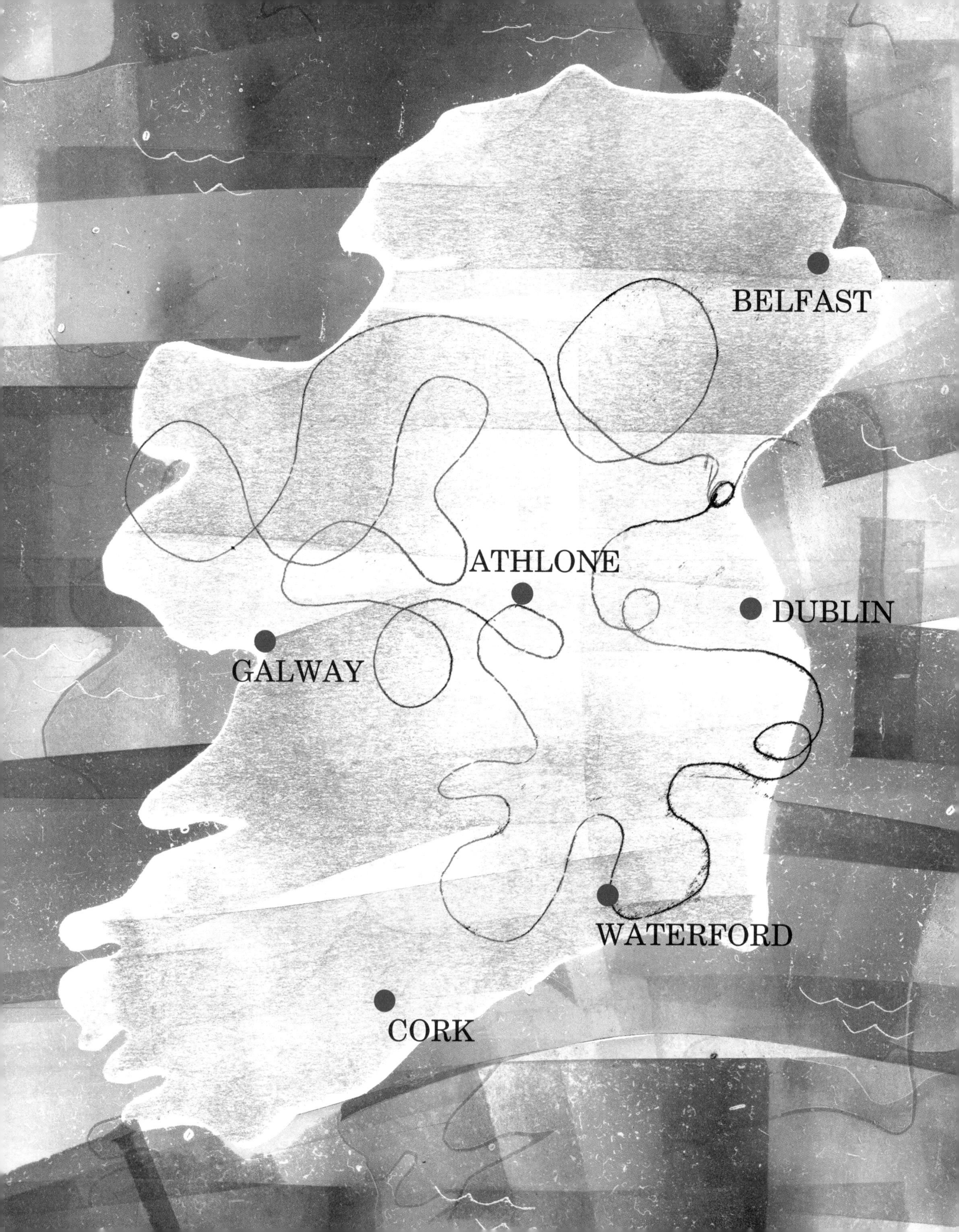

BELFAST

ATHLONE

DUBLIN

GALWAY

WATERFORD

CORK

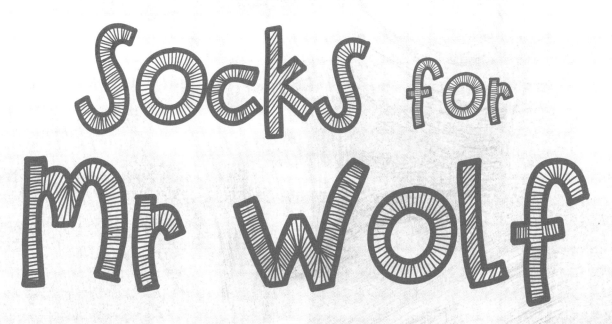

Socks for Mr Wolf

A WOOLLY ADVENTURE
AROUND IRELAND

Tatyana feeney

THE O'BRIEN PRESS
DUBLIN

Whose socks are these?

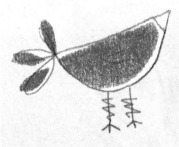

Do they belong to

the bird,

the turtle,

the cat?

No! These socks belong
to Mr Wolf.

Mr Wolf loved his socks.

They were cosy. They were colourful.

Mr Wolf felt taller
when he wore them.

They made him feel like dancing.

'Uh oh! A hole!'

It was only a small hole. Mr Wolf carried on as normal and HOPED no one would notice the hole ...

getting bigger

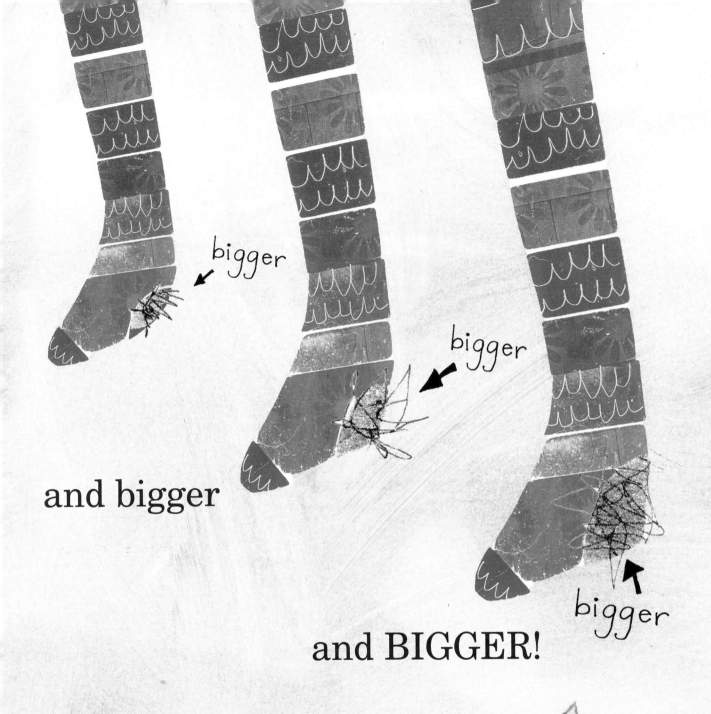

bigger

bigger

and bigger

bigger

and BIGGER!

Mr Wolf thought he could mend the hole.

Plasters didn't work.

Sticky tape didn't work.

Glue *definitely* didn't work!

NOTHING WAS WORKING!!

Then Mr Wolf had an idea ...

... maybe A BOOK would help?

Socks 101

Everything you ever wanted to know

wool for Amateurs

100 Socks to Knit

Mr Wolf strode out of the library full of plans for beautiful socks, every length and colour ...

'Some wool!
Just what
I was
looking
for!'

he thought.

Avoca Forest

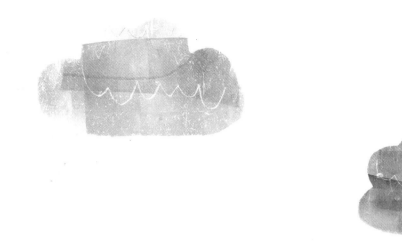

Lost in his book, Mr Wolf
followed the wool ...

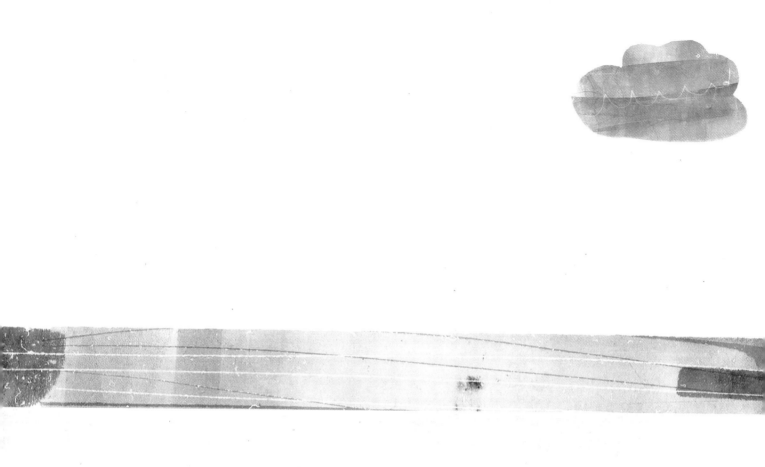

He followed it along the beach ...

through the city ...

'Imagine what I
can knit with all
this wool!'
he thought.

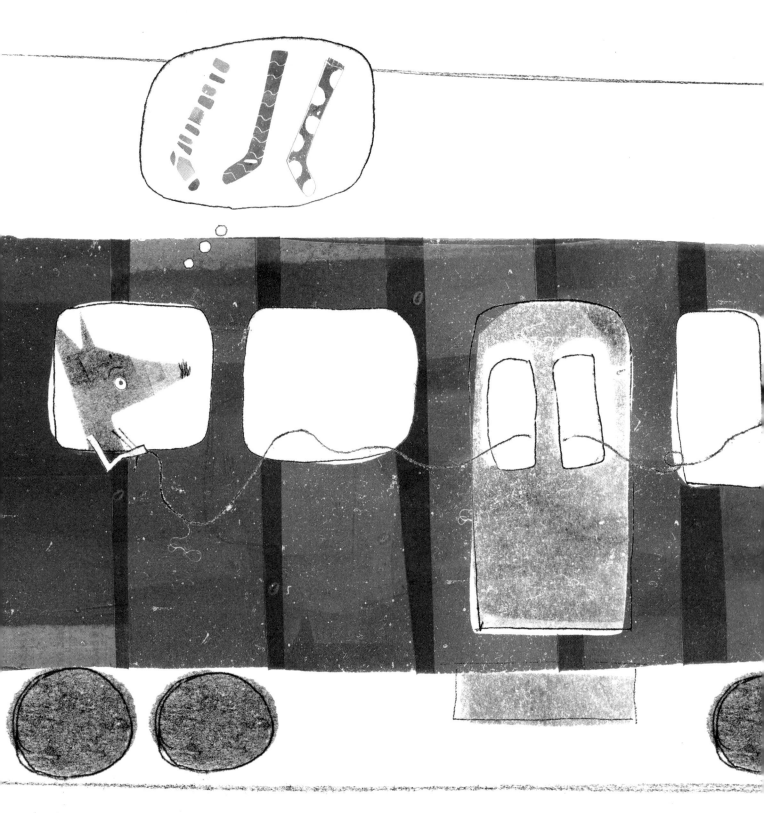

Mr Wolf followed the wool onto a train.
After all his walking ...

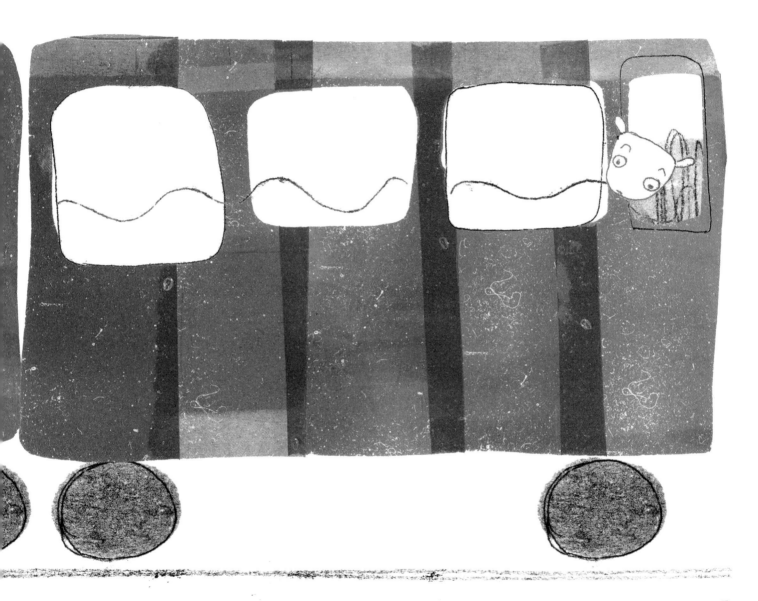

... he was glad to sit down and relax and think of all the things he could knit.

But when he got off the train he discovered that the end of the wool was attached to ...

... a sheep!

'Baa!'

26

'I'm sorry! Don't be scared,
I just wanted a little wool!'

cried Mr Wolf.

'Oh! Well, I was getting too warm anyway!'

said the sheep.

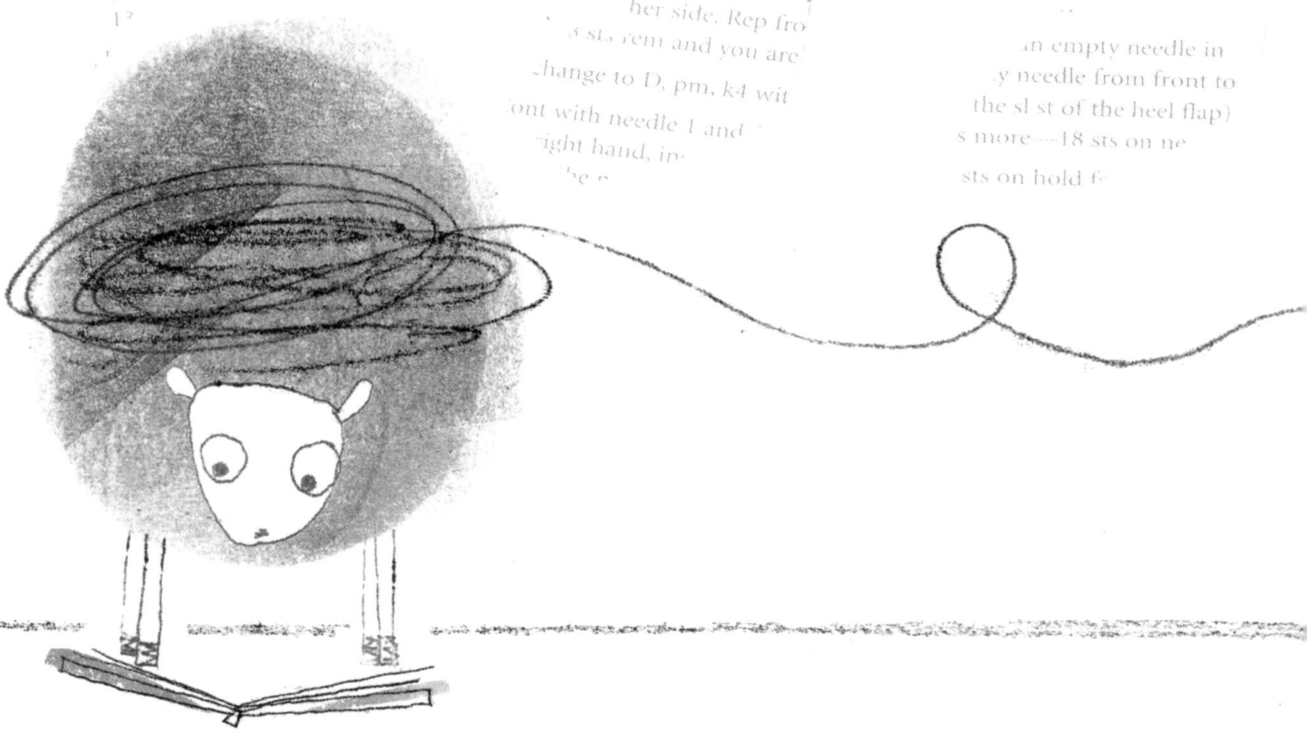

Mr Wolf was quite a good knitter and soon had a beautiful new pair of socks

– two in fact, in case of holes.

TATYANA FEENEY grew up in North Carolina, where she spent much of her childhood reading and drawing. This developed into a love of art and particularly illustrations in children's books, so she gave up her ambition to be a fire-girl and studied art history and illustration.

Tatyana now lives in Co. Meath with her husband and two children. She has illustrated several books in the O'Brien Press Panda series and is also the author and illustrator of *Small Bunny's Blue Blanket*, *Little Owl's Orange Scarf*, *Little Frog's Tadpole Trouble* and *Small Elephant's Bathtime*.

To Alex, who has always loved socks!

First published 2017 by The O'Brien Press Ltd,
12 Terenure Road East, Rathgar, Dublin 6, D06 HD27, Ireland
Tel: +353 1 4923333; Fax: +353 1 4922777
E-mail: books@obrien.ie
Website: www.obrien.ie
The O'Brien Press is a member of Publishing Ireland.

ISBN: 978-1-84717-906-7

6 5 4 3 2 1
20 19 18 17

Printed and bound in Poland by Białostockie Zakłady Graficzne S.A.
The paper in this book is produced using pulp from managed forests.

Published in

DUBLIN
UNESCO
City of Literature

Socks for Mr Wolf receives financial
assistance from the Arts Council